Escape From Egypt

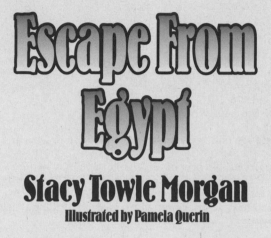

Stacy Towle Morgan

Illustrated by Pamela Querin

BETHANY HOUSE PUBLISHERS
MINNEAPOLIS, MINNESOTA 55438

Published by Bethany House Publishers
A Ministry of Bethany Fellowship, Inc.
11300 Hampshire Avenue South
Minneapolis, Minnesota 55438

Printed in the United States of America.

Library of Congress Cataloging-in-Publication Data

Morgan, Stacy Towle.
    Escape from Egypt / Stacy Towle Morgan.
        p. m . —(Ruby Slippers School ; 3)
    Summary: While visiting Cairo, nine-year-old Hope makes new friends of the Muslim faith and prays that they will discover the benefits of Christianity.
    [1. Cairo (Egypt)—Fiction. 2. Egypt—Fiction. 3. Christian life—Fiction.] I. Title. II. Series. III. Series: Morgan, Stacy Towle. Ruby Slippers School ; 3.
PZ7.M82642Es   1996
[Fic]—dc20   96–25229
ISBN 1–55661–602–3   CIP
                                                              AC

To the *real* Fouad—
who has been to
the desert and back.

Ruby Slippers School

9607

STACY TOWLE MORGAN has been writing ever since she was eight, when she set up a typewriter in the closet of the room she shared with her sister. A graduate of Cedarville College and Western Kentucky University, Stacy has written many feature articles and several books for children. Stacy and her husband, Michael, make their home in Indiana, where she currently spends her days home-schooling their four school-aged children in their own Ruby Slippers School.

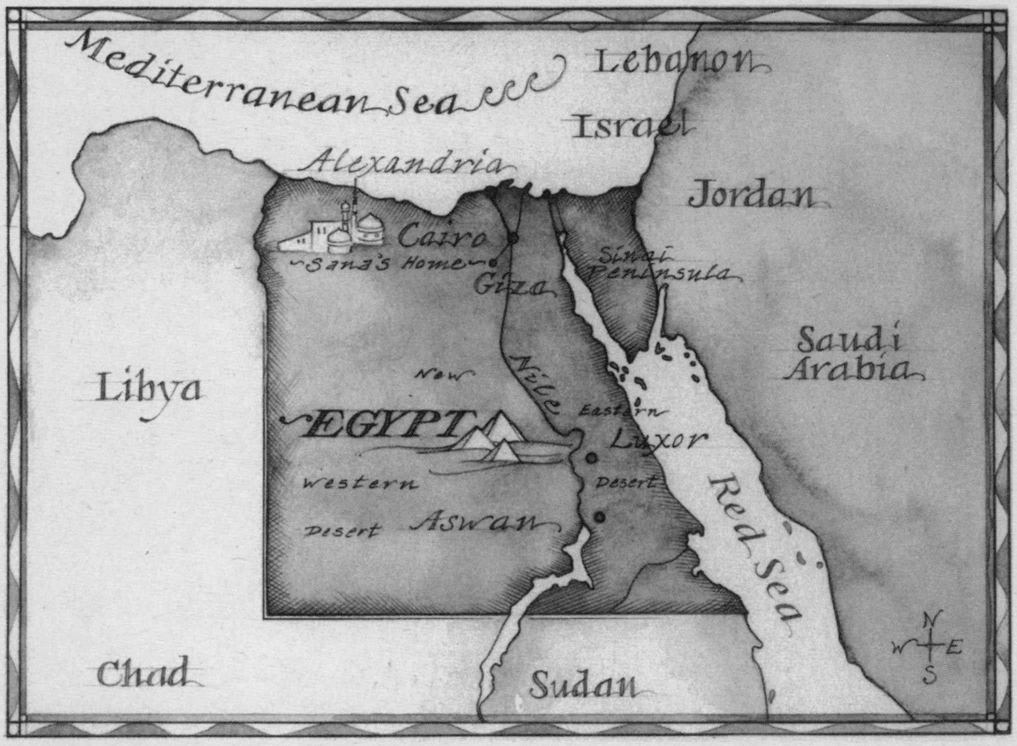
Mediterranean Sea
Lebanon
Israel
Alexandria
Jordan
Cairo
Sana's Home
Giza
Sinai
Peninsula
Saudi
Arabia
Libya
Nile
New
EGYPT
Eastern
Luxor
Western
Desert
Desert
Aswan
Red Sea
Chad
Sudan
N
W
E
S

Prologue

My name is Hope Vivian Brown. Last year, I asked for a cat for my eighth birthday, but I didn't get one. My little sister, Annie, asked for a cat for her birthday, too. She didn't get one either.

Someday I'm going to have a cat of my own—a black cat with a white spot on her nose. That way, if she eats anything she shouldn't, I'll be able to tell. Mom says whenever *I* wear anything white, she can always tell what I had for supper!

But I don't think my parents will ever let me have a cat. We travel all the time, so we can't have a pet. "Who would take care of her while we are gone?" Mom and Dad ask.

They're probably right. You see, Mom and Dad teach us at home. And when Dad has a business trip, he sometimes takes all of us with him. We get to go all over the world!

Just wait until you hear about our latest trip to Cairo, Egypt!

P.S. I still want a cat for my *next* birthday!

Chapter One

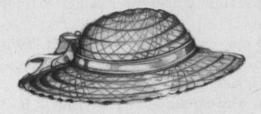

Annie, your hat!" I yelled, stepping off the bus in downtown Cairo. It was too late. Annie's hat had flown off with the wind and was blowing down the crowded sidewalk.

Dad ran after it. "I'll get it. You wait here."

We watched as he disappeared into the mass of people.

"I hope he finds his way back," Mom said.

"And I hope he finds my hat," cried Annie.

Annie and I had both gotten new hats for our trip to Egypt.

"I think you would have been better off with a turban—like that man over there." I laughed. We stared at the white cloth twisted like a braid around the man's head. "No chance of losing *that* hat in a windstorm."

As the man walked past us, I stared. He had on a long, black robe with flowing sleeves. He looked crisp and clean in the middle of this dusty city.

"Girls, you mustn't stare. It's very rude," Mom scolded. "Here comes your father. I think he has your hat."

Dad ran over to us, out of breath. "Whew, that was close," he said. "I almost had to bargain to get your hat back, Annie."

"But why would you have to buy it back? It belongs to me!" Annie complained.

"I guess Egyptians believe in 'finders keepers,'" Dad joked. He dabbed his forehead with a handkerchief.

"See that little handicapped boy by the side of that building?" He pointed to a mustard-colored building down the street. "He was sure your hat blew into his lap as a gift from Allah. I had to give him my magazine and key chain to get it back."

I looked down the street. I could barely see the boy as people pushed past between us.

"C'mon, girls. Let's get a taxi and get to our hotel."

Dad hailed a black-and-white taxi, and we climbed in. The driver piled our luggage in the trunk.

"Hold on to your hats, girls!" Dad warned. He says that every time we get into a taxi. This time, he really meant it!

Dad sat up front and the rest of us settled into the back. The driver didn't seem to notice the crowd of people in front of us. He drove right through them. There were many merchants and shoppers and donkeys carrying loads. There was even a woman with a basket of lemons on her head.

We whizzed past the handicapped boy. I saw his sad face for only a second. Maybe he wished he hadn't traded the hat, after all.

Chapter Two

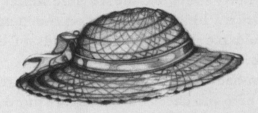

The taxi pulled up in front of an old building.
"Here's the hotel," Mom said. "Doesn't look like it's in the best part of town, Reid."

"It's the best I could do. I'll check it out in a minute. Just let me figure out what I need to pay the taxi driver first."

I looked at the meter in the front seat of the taxi. It showed the amount of money Dad should have to pay. "Mom, how come Dad has to figure out what to pay?" I asked. "It says what right there."

"Nothing is that easy in Egypt," Mom said. "Everyone assumes you will bargain. Dad knows what he is doing. Just watch."

Dad climbed out of the taxi and talked to the leather-skinned driver. Finally, Dad joined us on the curb.

"Well, I've haggled over prices two times already, and we've been in Cairo less than an hour," Dad said. He brushed the dust off his pants. "I'd say that's pretty good."

The noisy street told me we were still in the center of the city. I had never heard so much noise! My ears could barely take in the sounds of donkeys, chickens, car horns, and laughter.

Mom had to practically yell to be heard. "Let's duck in here and check in. We can see more of Cairo after we've unpacked."

Just as we started toward the door, a black cat with yellow eyes rushed past at top speed. He knocked Annie off her feet. "My hat," she yelled. "That cat has my hat!"

Sure enough, Annie's hat had landed on top of the cat. It hung from his collar. He looked a little like a black, furry cowboy as he raced away.

"That's just great!" Annie said. "Now I'll never see my hat again."

I helped her up and brushed the sand off her clothes. "It's OK, Annie. We can buy another hat. At least you're not hurt."

"Maybe you weren't meant to wear a hat on this trip, Annie," Dad chuckled.

"Everything is going wrong," she whimpered. "And now that a black cat ran in front of me, everything will keep going wrong."

"Hey, now," Mom said, wiping Annie's tears.

"We don't believe in superstitions like that. Try to think about good things. We're here, aren't we? Just last week you said you never thought we'd get here."

We stepped onto the cool, tile floor of the hotel lobby. A fan overhead made a gentle breeze. Annie and I sat on our suitcases while Mom and Dad checked in.

I leaned over to her and whispered, "Did you get a good look at that black cat?"

"No. Why?"

"Oh, nothing. It's just weird how it looked back at us, like it knew what it was doing. Really strange."

Just then, Dad motioned us to the elevator. We picked up our suitcases and walked in, and a man pulled metal crossbars across the front opening. It was the strangest elevator I had ever seen. A glass door closed in front of the bars, and the elevator jerked up.

We got off on the third floor. I don't think our room was what my mother expected.

"This looks pretty empty." Her voice echoed in the tiled room. It held only a wooden cabinet, a wooden double bed, and one brown chair.

"Wow, this leather chair sure is cracked," Annie said.

Dad opened the window, which was covered with iron bars. The street noise roared in. "Wouldn't you crack, too, if you had to listen to this every day?" he asked with a smile.

15

"This isn't funny, Reid." Mom seemed a little upset. "Where are the girls going to sleep?"

"Listen, honey," Dad said, "when I reserved the room, I wasn't sure the whole family would be able to come. This is just a little glitch. It'll work out."

"A little glitch? Not having a bed to sleep in is more than a little glitch!"

Dad walked into the bathroom and turned on the cold water. He splashed water on his face.

"There, now I feel better," he said, patting his face dry with a towel.

He gently took Mom's hands. "Gail, I plan to do two things right away. First, I'll call my friend Mo'yad. After that, I'll find another place to stay. I'm sorry if I upset you. I hope you'll forgive me."

Mom grinned. "You're pretty good at this bargaining stuff," she said. "I hope you'll forgive me, too."

They hugged.

Sometimes I think Annie and I are the only ones in our family who fight and have to work it out. It helps to know we aren't.

After Dad made the phone calls, he told us his friend Dr. Mo'yad Ibrahim had invited us to stay at his home. In fact, he was coming to pick us up in fifteen minutes!

"He even has a little girl about your age, Hope," Dad said. "I've never met her, but I'm sure that if she's anything like her dad, you'll get along great."

Chapter Three

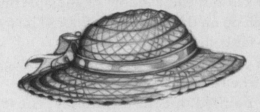

"L et me see if you still remember how to say an Egyptian hello, Reid, my friend." Dr. Ibrahim laughed as he and Dad kissed each other on each cheek, back and forth. "Peace be upon you."

"Upon you be peace and the mercy of God and his blessing," Dad replied. They both laughed and hugged.

"You haven't forgotten after all these years!" the doctor said, patting Dad on the back.

He turned to Annie and me. "So these are the lovely young women you told me about on the phone. Young ladies, I want you to meet my daughter, Sana. She is very excited about meeting you. Sana, meet Hope and Annie."

Sana smiled at us as her dad motioned for everyone to sit on the white couch. He handed us a tray of sweets.

"Help yourself," he said. "Grandma Salima will be in any moment with something to drink."

I looked out the window of the apartment. We were high up on the nineteenth floor. The whole city seemed far below.

"Do you like our city?" Sana asked. Her earrings jingled when she talked.

She pointed out the window. "Those round, pointed things you see on buildings are called *minarets*. Everywhere there is a minaret, there is a mosque where people worship. And, of course, way in the distance are the pyramids. Everyone who comes to Egypt wants to see them." Sana's voice jingled like her earrings. Her bright red dress with gold embroidery matched her cheerful smile.

Dr. Ibrahim was telling Mom and Dad a story. He and Dad had known each other in graduate school in the United States. But even then, Dr. Ibrahim had always planned to be a doctor in Egypt.

"Before my wife's death," he was saying, "I had everything a man could want, thanks be to God. I was doing well at work. We had a beautiful apartment, good friends, and a wonderful new baby . . . then my wife became ill. There was nothing I could do to cure her."

He stood as Grandma Salima came into the room with a tray of glasses. "But," he said loudly, "I

have been fortunate to have Sana's widowed Grandma to help me—and, of course, my little Sana." He pulled Sana into his lap. "Not so much a baby anymore, but still my little girl."

"Put the poor girl down," Grandma demanded. "She's nine years old, yet you treat her like a baby."

"As you can see," Dr. Ibrahim said, "I may be the doctor, but Grandma Salima is the ruler!"

"Pshaw, I know what I'm saying." Grandma Salima looked crossly at Sana. "Sana, look what I found on the floor by your bed." She held up a beautiful turquoise necklace with an Arabic word written on it. "Put it on right now. You mustn't go without it!"

"I'm afraid Grandma is as superstitious as they come," Dr. Ibrahim said. He picked up the necklace. "This necklace has the word *Allah* on it. It is supposed to keep away any harm that could come to Sana."

At that moment, a strange sound rang out in the city. I turned to look out the large picture window. From every minaret came a sing-songy sound—the Muslim call to worship. I knew what it was because I had read in my books about Muslims and the Muslim religion. Five times a day, Muslim people faced the city of Mecca, kneeled down, and touched their foreheads to the ground. They did this to obey their god, Allah.

I could see pockets of people kneeling where they were in the street. *Strange*, I thought. I couldn't imagine Americans stopping to kneel in the street and pray. We would get run over!

"What are they saying?" I asked.

"They're repeating a prayer called the *Sha'hada*."

"Do you do that?" I asked.

"Only if I'm with someone else who does. I don't really get into that stuff," Sana said, sounding bored.

I looked down again. I wondered how many of these people were just kneeling out of habit—or because their friends were.

"The Bible says to pray nonstop," I said. "If I did it this way, I'd have a hard time getting anything done!" I giggled.

Sana changed the subject. "What's your school like?" she asked.

I told her that we had school at home.

"We've been studying Egypt and Arabs in homeschool for almost a month now," I explained. "We knew Dad would be taking a trip to Egypt sometime soon, so we wanted to know more about this place."

"So tell me what you know," Sana said, her earrings jingling again.

I shared what I had read—that the people who live in Arab countries like Egypt are mainly Muslims. And that there are very few Christians. Muslims believe in a god called Allah, and they follow a prophet named Mohammed. They have read about

Jesus, but they don't understand that He died on the cross so they could have life forever in heaven with Him.

Sana looked uncomfortable. "I don't want to talk about this anymore," she said. "Let's go to my room and play dominoes."

Did I say something wrong? I thought. I'd ask Dad about it later.

Chapter Four

That evening, Dr. Ibrahim invited Annie and me to begin our school day at his clinic.

"You will see that Egyptians have the same problems you do," he said. "An American cold and an Egyptian cold sound the same—but the sneezes are thousands of miles apart!"

Dr. Ibrahim was very funny. I couldn't wait to visit him at the clinic. Sana was going to be in school tomorrow, so Annie and I wouldn't get to see her until dinnertime.

"If going to the clinic is school for Hope and Annie, why can't it be school for me, too?" she asked.

Dr. Ibrahim cupped her chin in his hand. "My little one, you are too smart for your own good! You must go to school. You will meet us afterward, as I said."

Sana nodded, but she didn't look too happy.

That night when we lay in bed, I listened again to the call to worship. It was hard to get used to that strange wailing sound.

"Annie, are you still awake?" I whispered.

"Yes, what do you want?"

"I don't think I'm used to the time difference yet. I can't fall asleep."

Annie propped herself up on one elbow. "I don't feel very well. I hope I'm not getting sick."

"Here, this will cheer you up." I picked up Ellsworth, my teddy bear, and wrapped a pair of my white leggings around his head in a turban.

"Welcome to Egypt," I said in the best Egyptian accent I could. "I am the Arab bear El-sworth."

We giggled.

"Maybe it would be easier to call him your *bear-ab*!" Annie snorted.

I took my flashlight out and shone the light in her face.

"Annie, your cheeks are all red!"

"Of course they're red. It's hot in this room!"

"You're probably right. We'd better get some rest. We've got lots to do tomorrow."

———

When I woke up the next morning, Annie was already up. "Hope, I have funny red splotches all over my stomach." She looked worried.

"It can't be the chicken pox. You've already had those," I said. "Did you tell Mom?"

"I'm going to now."

When Mom and Dad saw the rash, they knew right away what it was.

"It's called Fifth disease. It just so happens that your friend Susan had it right before we left for Egypt. I was afraid this would happen," Mom said.

Annie started to cry. "First the hat, and now this. I told you everything was going to go wrong, didn't I? It's all because of that black cat!"

"Now, Annie, stop it. Don't blame a black cat for something your friend Susan gave you. You'll just have to live with it until it's gone. The most contagious part is over, but you'll have to stay inside until you're feeling better," Mom said.

So Annie stayed at the apartment while Mom, Dr. Ibrahim, and I went to the clinic.

The clinic was only a short ride away, but it felt like we were in a different world. The streets weren't just crowded, they were packed! As we got out of the car, I looked up and saw two women leaning out their windows, yelling at each other. Below, a donkey carried a heavy load of trash. Behind him waddled a boy with four bolts of silk cloth. The whole city seemed to be overloaded.

Near the door of the clinic, I spotted someone I recognized—the handicapped boy! He was the same

one who had haggled with Dad over Annie's hat.

"Mom, it's him—the boy who had Annie's hat," I said.

Before she could answer, Dr. Ibrahim said to the boy, "Hello, As'ad. God be with you."

As'ad smiled and held out a cup. Dr. Ibrahim dropped in some coins.

"As'ad and five other boys beg for money in this area. I'm afraid his leader isn't very nice to him. I have had to bandage some bad wounds."

"What happens to him?" I asked.

"If he tries to get out of begging, he is whipped with a belt. His leader is that tall boy over there in the black pants. He used to be a beggar like As'ad before he took over this territory."

"What's wrong with As'ad?" Mom asked.

"What isn't wrong with As'ad?" Dr. Ibrahim said. "His father is dead, his mother is very poor and ill, and he is missing a leg below one knee. I treat his mother at the clinic for free. But I can't help him because the treatment costs too much money."

For the rest of the morning, we watched Dr. Ibrahim patiently work with the people who came in off the streets. Mom told me that he could work as the head of any hospital he chose. Instead, he preferred to work at the small clinic with his two partners, Dr. Mohsen and Dr. Muhammed.

"Dr. Ibrahim really cares about people," she

added. "I think it's because he was adopted when he was a little boy."

I hadn't heard that before. Dr. Ibrahim had been an orphan! Mom said he had been left in a basket on the steps of a very rich, childless family in Cairo. They took him.

"So they sent him to the United States for college?" I asked.

"Yes. He promised himself that when he finished school, he would come back to Egypt and help his people. As you can see, he does that every day."

Just then, a man came through the clinic door in a big hurry. He was out of breath. I couldn't understand what he wanted, but I heard him say Dr. Ibrahim's name. He glanced behind him nervously. Was someone chasing him?

Chapter Five

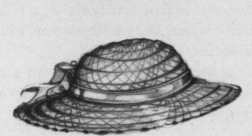

B efore anyone could stop the man, he was running down the hall opening doors. He opened one just as Dr. Ibrahim was coming out. The doctor quickly took him into his office and shut the door.

A few minutes later, Dr. Ibrahim came out and asked Mom and me to step into his office.

"Mrs. Brown, Hope, this is Fouad. He is a friend of mine and Reid's. We all went to school together."

Fouad spoke again—this time in perfect English. "Mr. Brown and I met at a campus Bible study. I can hardly believe God has brought us together once more. But then, our God is wonderful, isn't He?"

I wasn't sure if he was talking about Allah or my God. This was getting confusing!

Mom came right out and said it. "So you're a Christian?"

"Of course!" he said matter-of-factly. "Reid helped me to become a Christian."

Dr. Ibrahim was leaning against his desk, dragging the toe of one shoe across the floor. "Fouad, I have patients to see. Do you think you will be safe here for a while?"

"Yes, I am sorry for rambling. I am just so excited to see Christian friends. Please, go on with your work. I will wait here until you decide what to do."

I was curious now. Why was Fouad worried about being safe? What was Dr. Ibrahim going to do?

Dr. Ibrahim left and said he'd see us later. Mom told Fouad that we needed to leave now, too, but maybe we'd see him later that evening.

"Before you leave, I must tell you a secret," he said. "I am running from the authorities, the people who are in charge of Egypt. They don't know I'm here, but it won't take them long to find me—especially if Dr. Ibrahim's partners learn I'm here."

"I don't understand, Fouad," Mom said. "Why are you running?"

"The authorities know I am telling others about Jesus Christ. They know I give away Bibles and run a Bible study from my home. Tonight, they will break into my apartment to arrest me, but I won't be there."

"How horrible!" I said. "All because you are telling people about Jesus?"

"It's not allowed here. I am not supposed to tell others unless I am asked. But who can wait to be asked?"

I felt sick to my stomach. Maybe I was getting what Annie had. Or maybe it was because of what Fouad had said.

"So why are you worried about Dr. Ibrahim's partners?" I asked.

"They are angry that I believe in Christ. They are not happy that I have left my Egyptian-Muslim beliefs," Fouad said. "If they knew I was here, they'd take me to the authorities themselves."

"But what about Dr. Ibrahim?" Mom asked. "Does he feel the same way?"

"No, there isn't a bit of hate in Dr. Ibrahim's bones. In fact, I sometimes think he's this close to becoming a Christian himself." Fouad held his thumb and forefinger close together. "Who knows, maybe God brought us all together to help that happen. It wouldn't surprise me."

We said goodbye and walked out to catch a taxi. As'ad was gone, but not his stool. And on it was the black cat!

He looked at me as if to say, "What are you staring at?"

I ran to the curb where Mom was standing.

"Mom, look! It's the black cat that knocked over Annie and stole her hat."

Mom looked. The cat was gone.

"Are you sure, Hope? All black cats look alike, if you ask me."

"Not this one, Mom. I'm sure it was the one who stole Annie's hat."

"He didn't steal the hat, Hope. It just got caught on his collar," she said. "You make him sound like a person."

I was beginning to wonder.

Chapter Six

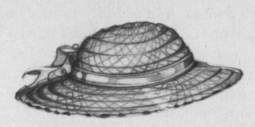

That night at dinner, Dad, Dr. Ibrahim, and Fouad talked about college.

"Tell us the one about the bottle rockets in your sock drawer again," I said.

"I'm afraid I've told that one too many times," Dad said.

Mom agreed.

"I could use some rockets to cast out spirits," Grandma Salima declared. "Your Annie doesn't look much better tonight. Maybe she is cursed."

Poor Annie! I asked if I could be excused to visit her. "I'll be back as soon as I can," I said to Sana. We were going to make plans to go to the pyramids tomorrow. Sana was able to skip school to go.

I walked down the hall to the bedroom and knocked quietly on the door.

"All the evil spirits are gone," Annie said. "And if you're a genie, go away."

I walked in. "What are you talking about?"

"*You* should have been here all day with Grandma Salima. You'd understand then," Annie said with a pout. "She's crazy! She moved me from room to room while she cleared out all the 'evil spirits' from the place. If you ask me, the smell in the kitchen should have been enough to get rid of them! *I* sure wanted to leave!"

"It couldn't have been that bad," I said.

"It was. I really missed all of you. Things got so bad I started talking to Ellsworth, the bear-ab!" She started to smile.

I sat down on the bed and told her about what had happened at the clinic—and about the cat.

"Do you think the cat belongs to As'ad?" Annie asked.

"I don't know, but I'm going to find out," I answered. "But now, I'm supposed to let you get some rest."

"Just what I want to do—lie here and look at the ceiling."

I headed out the door. Then I peeked my head back into the room. "Hey, I know what you've got. It's the Egyptian plague!"

Annie just missed me with her pillow.

The next morning, we left early for our trip to the pyramids. Dr. Ibrahim was going to drive since it was his day off.

Fouad was coming along, too. He had decided the last place the authorities would look for him was a tourist trap like the Pyramids of Giza.

Mom stayed with Annie. Mom wasn't about to let Annie stay alone again in the apartment with Grandma Salima.

On the way there, I asked Sana if she got to ride camels often.

"Are you kidding?" she said. "Why would I ride on a stinky camel when I can sit in my dad's fancy car?"

"Oh," I replied. I looked out the window at the desert ahead.

"I guess riding one can be fun—once in a while," Sana said. She must have been worried about hurting my feelings. "But I wouldn't want to do it every day. It's a pretty rough ride."

We were getting close now. I could see the tip of the Great Pyramid. Slowly, the tip of the second pyramid appeared. As we pulled into the parking lot, I caught sight of the last of the three pyramids—and the Great Sphinx. The sphinx was huge! With the head of a man and the body of a lion, it looked like something out of a fairy tale.

"We'll just park over by the rest house and find a camel or two to rent," Dr. Ibrahim suggested.

I looked at the swirls the wind made in the desert sand. You could almost see the heat.

"It's going to be a hot day," Fouad said.

"Don't forget to cover your head so you don't get sunburned, Hope." Sana handed me a scarf and showed me how to wrap it around my head and shoulders. I felt like an actress from an Arabian Nights movie.

As we stepped up to the camels, the wind shifted. "Phew," I said, holding my nose. "You were right. Give me the smell of car leather over a camel any day."

Robed men with turbans helped to lift us up onto the kneeling camels. The camels' back legs rose first. I felt like I was going to topple onto the ground. Then the camel rose on its front legs, and everything evened out.

"Hold on to your hats, girls," Dad said. "It's going to be a bumpy ride!"

He was right.

As I rode, I thought about the wise men riding their camels to see baby Jesus. A Promised Land would have seemed pretty far away out here in this heat. It was easy to picture Bible stories here in Egypt where so many of them had happened.

After a long morning of sightseeing, we headed back to the rest house for a picnic.

"There is so much history here for Christians to

enjoy," Dad said. "It's hard to believe that Egypt is a Muslim nation."

"We believe the Bible, too," Dr. Ibrahim defended. "But it is the Koran we really study. Are you still praying for me to get me to know this Christ of yours, Reid?"

Dr. Ibrahim handed Sana a piece of pita bread called *K'ak*. "Sana, what do you think of this Christianity?"

Sana quietly turned away from her father. She stared out at the giant pyramids.

Looking at Fouad, Dr. Ibrahim said, "I'm afraid my lack of faith has caused Sana not to believe in anything."

Sana put down her food. "I want to know why Allah let my mother die. Doesn't he want me to be happy? Doesn't he know how lonely I feel without a mother?"

"Jesus knows what it's like to be separated from someone He loves," Dad said. "He loves you, even though you are not yet a part of His family."

All was quiet as Sana stared out at the desert, her back to us.

She turned, and there was a tear in her eye. "How could Jesus love me? I haven't done anything for Him."

"Don't you see, Sana?" Fouad began. "Jesus doesn't love you because of what you do for Him.

He loves you because He is love—He died on the cross for you."

Sana moved closer to her father. "I don't understand . . . but I want to."

"I know, Sana," he said.

Just then, a car squealed into the parking lot. Someone called Dr. Ibrahim's name.

"It's my assistant at the clinic," he said. "I wonder what could be wrong?"

Chapter Seven

D r. Ibrahim! Dr. Ibrahim! It is an emergency. As'ad's mother has become very ill. Her temperature is very high, and she keeps asking for you," the assistant said.

The doctor looked concerned. "Sana, you stay here with the others. I will go back to the clinic with Walid."

"It's OK, friend. We'll take Sana home in your car," Dad said. "But now, I think we'd all rather go back to the clinic to make sure As'ad's mother is all right. Someone might need to help As'ad."

If something happens to As'ad's mother, he won't have any family left, I thought suddenly. *As'ad would be an orphan like Dr. Ibrahim was.*

We followed Walid's car back to the clinic. It didn't seem to matter how loudly we honked the horn as we tried to squeeze between the other cars. Our horn couldn't be heard above all the other honking horns.

At last, we got back to the clinic. We saw As'ad sitting outside on his stool, rocking back and forth, sobbing. He was holding the black cat in his arms and stroking its back.

The men went inside. Sana and I squatted next to As'ad. We tried to comfort him. Sana had to do all the talking since he didn't speak English.

I stared helplessly at the black cat with the yellow eyes.

"Ask him what his cat's name is," I said to Sana.

"This is Antar," she answered without asking. "He is everyone's cat. Loved by all. Owned by none."

"He knocked over my sister when we got out of the taxi last Tuesday," I explained.

"Well, wasn't she lucky!" Sana said. "Cats are very special in Egypt. Cats have always had a special place in Egyptian history."

She's right, I thought, remembering the books I had read. Ancient Egypt had had a cat god named Bastet. Pharaohs would even have their cats mummified and buried with them. Cats were good luck in Egypt—if you believed in luck.

"I'll have to tell Annie when we get home," I said. "She'll be happy to hear that."

"I don't know when we'll be going home," Sana

said. "It could be a long time before As'ad's mother gets better."

The sun was low now. It wouldn't be long before another call to prayer.

Dad opened the door to the clinic and asked Sana to bring As'ad in. "It's time for him to say goodbye to his mother," he said in English.

No! I thought. I felt terrible. I was glad As'ad couldn't understand what Dad was saying.

"Why don't you girls wait just inside the door. I think it would be better if I carried As'ad into the room myself."

The clinic smelled like rubbing alcohol. I felt sick to my stomach again.

"Why do people have to die?" Sana burst out. "It doesn't make sense."

I put my arm around her. Right then, the call to prayer began. I said my own prayer. "Please be with As'ad, Lord. And please help Sana to understand what it means to follow you. Amen."

I looked down at my charm bracelet. It wasn't anything like Sana's necklace. It wasn't made to keep away evil spirits. I thought about my friend Philippe in Belgium. I prayed that he would follow Jesus, too. I had so many people to pray for. Five times a day could never even be enough! I really *did* need to pray without stopping.

At that moment, Dr. Ibrahim stepped into the waiting room. "I am afraid that As'ad's mother has died. This will be very hard for him. Now he has no one to take care of him." He shook his head.

"I told Allah, 'I will make a deal with you. Let me save As'ad's mother, and I will pray five times a day and be a good Muslim.' He did not listen. This is not fair to As'ad. It just isn't fair."

Dr. Ibrahim walked down the hall to his office.

"Poor *baba*," Sana said. "He tries so hard to help people. He hates to see them hurting."

Fouad came out carrying As'ad in his arms. The boy had cried himself to sleep.

"He must be so tired," Fouad said. "I see he has been beaten again." He pointed to the calf of his one whole leg. It had a red strap mark on it.

"I think we should take him home," Sana said. "What's another guest? Most apartments in Cairo are standing room only!

"Wouldn't As'ad be surprised to open his eyes in the guest bedroom?" she went on. "We must do it. Fouad, you wouldn't mind sharing a room, would you?" she asked.

"I'm afraid I cannot stay tonight, my friend," he said sadly. "I ran into your father's partner Dr. Mohsen when we came back to the clinic. He spit on me and threatened to tell the authorities where I am. I need to escape tonight."

Dr. Ibrahim appeared around the corner. "Where will you go?"

"I have a plane ticket to America. A friend of

mine has offered to help me get a job. I have left my apartment and all my things. I will go with what I have on my back. There is a little money in my pocket."

Dr. Ibrahim looked angry. "That's just wonderful," Dr. Ibrahim said. "It's just like you Christians to leave us when the going gets tough. How do you think others will hear about this Jesus of yours if you leave? Someone has to stay and tell them!"

"I think it is time someone else takes that job," Fouad said. He looked straight at Dr. Ibrahim.

"What are you looking at me for? I'm a Muslim, remember?"

"Yes, I remember," Fouad said with a smile.

Chapter Eight

As'ad was still asleep when we got back to the apartment. Dr. Ibrahim quietly tucked him into the guest bed. In the morning, we would surprise him with bean soup and fresh fruit, he said. It wouldn't take away the hurt of losing his mother, but we would all do our best to comfort him.

Annie was feeling better. Her rash was almost gone. Mom said she could go out in the morning since her fever was gone, too.

"I can't believe that cat story," Annie said. "I guess I was silly to be superstitious about a black cat. A few days with Grandma Salima sure have shown me how ridiculous it is to be superstitious."

That night, there was a loud knock at the door.

Dr. Ibrahim answered. It was the secret police! They were looking for Fouad and had heard he was staying with us.

"No, he is not here," Dr. Ibrahim said honestly. "He is a friend of mine, but I haven't seen him to-night."

"Do you mind if we check your apartment?" they asked. I don't think they would have taken no for an answer.

As they started down the hallway, Sana blocked the door to the guest bedroom. "Don't go in there," she said. "A little boy is sleeping."

The police went in anyway. They pulled back the covers. There lay poor As'ad, curled up in a little ball.

"They never trust anyone, these secret police," Sana whispered to me.

I shook my head.

After the police had left, Mom and Dad came in to say good-night to Annie and me. I gave Mom a long hug.

"Well, what was that for?" she asked.

"Just because," I said. I could feel my throat tighten.

"Hope, are you OK?" she asked. "I know it's been a rough day for all of us."

"Oh, Momma," I sobbed. "I don't want you to die!"

"Oh, sweetie, I'm not going to die. Not now, anyway," she said.

I pulled away from her. "But you are going to die someday, right?"

"Well, we are all going to die someday, Hope."

"But we'll see each other again in heaven, right?"

"That's right. That's the best part about being a Christian. God promises that we will be in heaven with Him when we die. And everyone who believes in Him will be in heaven together."

"But what about Dr. Ibrahim and Sana and As'ad? I want them to be in heaven with us."

"God wants them to be in heaven, too, honey. We can do our part to tell them that, but God has to do the rest."

The last call to prayer started just then. "Let's pray together right now that God will open their hearts to Him."

Chapter Nine

T he next morning at the breakfast table, something seemed different. Dr. Ibrahim and Sana
were sitting with an open Bible. It looked like my
Dad's.

"Where did you get that?" I asked.

"It is your father's Bible. We were reading the
New Testament, what we call the *Injeel*," said the
doctor. "It has some very interesting stories about
Jesus in it."

"Yes, it does," I said.

"I'm afraid I spent so many years reading the
Koran, I never bothered to read much of the Bible.
It's a shame that it took me so long."

I tried not to get too excited. As we talked, the
rest of the family joined us at the table.

Annie was looking a lot better. "Is As'ad awake?"

"He is now," Sana answered.

We all turned to see Dad carrying As'ad in his arms. As'ad looked a bit puzzled, but he smiled when he recognized Dr. Ibrahim.

"I have an announcement to make," Dr. Ibrahim said as he stood up and took As'ad in his arms. "I've decided to adopt As'ad."

As Sana translated, As'ad's eyes lit up.

"He will be my son, a part of our family."

Sana grinned and patted As'ad on the back. "Welcome to our home."

Already he looked like a different person. He had been bathed and dressed in new clothes. As'ad did not look worried anymore as he hungrily ate his breakfast.

Just then, Grandma Salima came in with more breakfast food. "I don't know what you want with another child. I'm the one who must care for him, and his mother not dead for more than twenty-four hours. It is not good. I feel the spirits are not happy," she said.

She walked over to Dr. Ibrahim. "And look at you," Grandma Salima went on. "Why are you reading that book?" She pointed to the Bible. "Better the Koran than the Bible, if you ask me."

"Grandma Salima, please. We have guests," Sana said.

"Yes, yes. It's always *my* fault. I not only feed guests and take care of them, now I upset them," she muttered as she went back into the kitchen.

"Please excuse her," Dr. Ibrahim said. "She's had quite a day with the news of the adoption and all. She'll be better tomorrow."

"Mom, Dad?" I asked when we had finished breakfast. "Can Annie and I go to the clinic with Dr. Ibrahim? Annie hasn't seen it yet. I could show her around." I secretly hoped we might see the black cat, too.

Sure enough, when we got out of the car, Antar was perched on As'ad's stool. He looked like he had been waiting for us. And under the stool was Annie's hat!

"Look, Annie!" I said. "He brought back your hat."

Dr. Ibrahim bent down to pet the cat. "So this is the famous lost hat. Wonder how it got here. It's hard to tell with Antar. Wonder if he misses As'ad. Maybe he'd like a home with him in our apartment."

"Are you serious?" I said. "That would be great!"

"Just what that apartment needs." Annie smirked. "Grandma Salima *and* a black cat."

Inside the clinic, it was quiet. It was still early for patients, but Dr. Ibrahim's two partners were already there. In fact, they were standing right by the door.

"Hello, Dr. Ibrahim," said Dr. Muhammed. "We hear you are hanging around Christians lately."

Both men stood with their arms crossed.

"We hear that you may even be a Christian yourself. Is this true, Doctor?"

Dr. Ibrahim stood straight and tall. "This is true," he said.

I gasped. How come he hadn't told us? Why was he telling these men who were so angry at Christians?

"If this is the case, then you must leave now. This is what comes of befriending Fouad. Get out! All of you Christians, get out!"

Dr. Ibrahim quickly led us back out to the car. As he came around to the driver's side, he stopped. "I'm afraid we'll have to walk, girls. All of my tires are flat."

I couldn't believe it! Dr. Ibrahim probably had only been a Christian for a few hours, but people were already making life hard for him. But his angry partners and the flat tires didn't seem to bother him. He looked peaceful as we moved through the crowd.

"You sure don't have any problem finding your way around here," I said as Annie and I ran to keep up with him.

"The trick is to remember where you're headed and try not to be distracted," he said.

"But there's so much to look at."

"I have seen it all many times before," he replied.

Somehow I got the feeling he was talking about something other than our walk through the market.

"Wait a minute!" Annie yelled out. "We need to go back! We forgot to bring the cat!"

"It's too late now," Dr. Ibrahim said. "We cannot go back. We can never go back."

"But it would have been so nice to bring the cat home to As'ad," she said.

Just then, there was a commotion ahead of us. A store owner was yelling as a young man darted from the store.

Dr. Ibrahim gently pushed us against one of the buildings and ran after him. He came back a few minutes later, wiping his forehead with a handkerchief.

"What happened?" I asked.

He told us that the young boy had stolen some jewelry from a merchant. When the merchant yelled out, several passersby ran after the boy and caught him before the police could.

"You see, in our city, we work together. You can be sure that if you go astray, someone will catch you."

That's the way it was for Fouad, I thought. The Egyptian Muslims thought it was wrong to be a Christian, so they had chased Fouad out of the country.

Would Dr. Ibrahim have to leave, too?

Chapter Ten

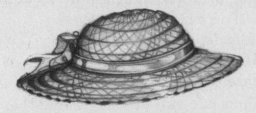

When we got back to the apartment, there was a phone message from Fouad.

"He wants you to call him back," Dad said.

As Dr. Ibrahim went to make the call, Annie and I told Mom and Dad about what had happened while we were gone.

"Well, we sure have a surprise for you," Mom said.

"You just have to promise that you won't read too much into this," said Dad.

"Read too much into what?" I asked.

"Look who's here." They guided us over to the couch.

There on the white couch lay Antar!

"How did *you* get here?" Annie asked.

"Are you expecting an answer?" Mom laughed.

"I can't believe it," I said. "It's so weird how this cat got here beforc we did! How did he find us?"

Antar just lay there, squinting his eyes.

"Well, Grandma Salima is thrilled," Dad said. "She's sure that everything will work out right now that they have a black cat in the house."

Dr. Ibrahim came out of his room. "Well, Fouad is fine. He's settled down in New York City for now and is already inviting everyone he knows to come and visit."

"That's a big place," Dad said. "In some ways, it's not a lot different than Cairo."

Dr. Ibrahim sat down on the couch. "Well, well, what is this? Antar wasn't willing to wait to be found."

He stroked the cat, but the look on his face turned serious.

"I am very concerned," he said. "I don't know if we can stay in Cairo any longer.

"Early this morning at the call to prayer, I looked out at my people, bowing to Allah. I realized I needed this Christ of yours—not a god who seems so far away. I chose to become a Christian. I understand now what Fouad has been telling me all along."

"Why are you worried, then?" Dad asked.

"I am such a new Christian. Should I stay here and risk losing everything, or should I go to the United States where being a Christian is so easy?"

"I can't answer that for you, Dr. Ibrahim," Dad said. "But I can tell you that being a Christian in the United States is not that easy. Many people in our country don't want to hear about Jesus, either."

Dad went on. "Maybe you need to look at the story of Moses for your answer. He left his palace in Egypt and went out into the desert. Of course, he had different reasons for leaving. But in the end, he returned to Egypt, and God used him to help his people."

"Do you think I need to go out to the desert?" Dr. Ibrahim asked.

"No, but maybe you need to spend some time preparing yourself before you face the people of Cairo again as a Christian. It's kind of like when you studied medicine in the States and then came back here to work."

"This I will think about," Dr. Ibrahim said. "I know that my heart is in Cairo. I care for my people. I have cured many here. Still, there was always something missing. I could not give them what they really needed. Jesus is the only one who can heal the heart."

Dad sat awhile with Dr. Ibrahim and talked. Mom took us back to the room to help us pack our bags. We needed to leave soon to go to the airport.

"I can't believe I hardly got to see anything," Annie complained. "We've been in Egypt for days and the only thing I got to study was the design on my bedspread."

"I'm sorry you were sick, Annie," I said. "But when we get home, you'll have some great stories to tell about Grandma Salima!"

"Girls, make sure you pack everything," Mom said. "We are going to pick up Sana at school on the way to the airport. She wants to say goodbye herself."

"At least it won't be lonely for her with As'ad around," Annie said.

I placed Ellsworth in the top of my pack. "Everyone needs a friend. Dr. Ibrahim says that with some physical therapy, As'ad might be able to walk again. All he needs is an artificial leg."

I secretly hoped that Dr. Ibrahim, Sana, and As'ad would come home on the plane with us.

"Mom . . . I'm worried about our friends. Will they be OK after we leave? Maybe we never should have come in the first place."

"Of course we should have come," Mom said. "God has used this whole trip. Now Dr. Ibrahim is a Christian! God will take care of him and his family."

I nodded.

We said goodbye to As'ad and Grandma Salima. Annie tipped her hat to the black cat as we walked out the door. "Hats off to a great cat!" she said. "I'm going to miss you."

At the front of the apartment building, a limousine was waiting for us. "Wow!" I said. "I've never ridden in one of these before."

Dr. Ibrahim opened the door. "Step right in. I thought you might like to go in style."

Dad was shocked. "You didn't need to do this, Dr. Ibrahim."

"Of course I didn't," he said. "But I wanted to."

When we picked up Sana at school, she smiled. "Sure beats a camel ride!"

We exchanged addresses and promised to write to each other when we got home.

"Be careful what you say in your letters, though," she warned. "Sometimes someone else reads them before I do."

"Your dad?"

"No, silly. You remember those policemen who came to our house a few nights ago? Well, they don't just search houses."

I shivered. It was scary to think of people going through your mail. I was looking forward to going home.

Then Sana handed me a package. "This is a little something for you, Hope. For your bracelet."

She handed Annie a present, too.

Annie opened hers first. "Oh, it's beautiful, Sana," she said. She held up an orange silk scarf.

"It's some of the best silk made," Sana said. "I thought the color would look really good with your strawberry blond hair. Now open yours, Hope."

Inside the box was a beautiful silver cross. Sana took my hand. "I know this isn't a good luck charm. I just wanted you to know that I have decided to become a part of God's family, too. So I guess we're related!"

I couldn't believe it! I never expected our trip would turn out this way when we got off the bus our first day in Cairo. My prayers for Sana had already been answered!

That afternoon, as our plane flew over the huge Sahara Desert, I stared out at the emptiness. I knew things were going to be rough for Dr. Ibrahim and his family from now on. They would feel so alone. But I also knew that God would take care of them.

High up in the air, we couldn't hear the call to prayer anymore. But I prayed anyway. I knew God was listening.

The End

Series for Young Readers*
From Bethany House Publishers

★ ★ ★

BACKPACK MYSTERIES
by Mary Carpenter Reid

This excitement-filled mystery series follows the mishaps and adventures of Steff and Paulie Larson as they strive to help often-eccentric relatives crack their toughest cases.

★ ★ ★

THE CUL-DE-SAC KIDS
by Beverly Lewis

Each story in this lighthearted series features the hilarious antics and predicaments of nine endearing boys and girls who live on Blossom Hill Lane.

★ ★ ★

RUBY SLIPPERS SCHOOL
by Stacy Towle Morgan

Join the fun as home-schoolers Hope and Annie Brown visit fascinating countries and meet inspiring Christians from around the world!

★ ★ ★

THE THREE COUSINS DETECTIVE CLUB™
by Elspeth Campbell Murphy

Famous detective cousins Timothy, Titus, and Sarah-Jane learn compelling Scripture-based truths while finding—and solving—intriguing mysteries.